My Weird

Mrs. Marge Is in Charge!

Dan Gutman

Pictures by
Jim Paillot

HARPER
An Imprint of HarperCollinsPublishers

To Issie Templeton

My Weirdtastic School #5: Mrs. Marge Is in Charge!
Text copyright © 2024 by Dan Gutman
Illustrations copyright © 2024 by Jim Paillot

Library of Congress Control Number: 2023943862
ISBN 978-0-06-320711-0 (pbk bdg) — ISBN 978-0-06-320712-7 (trade bdg)

Typography by Laura Mock
24 25 26 27 28   PC/CWR   10 9 8 7 6 5 4 3 2 1

First Edition

Contents

TO THE READER:
This is the first My Weird School book to be written
with the help of artificial intelligence (AI).*

---

*"Not really, but let's pretend."

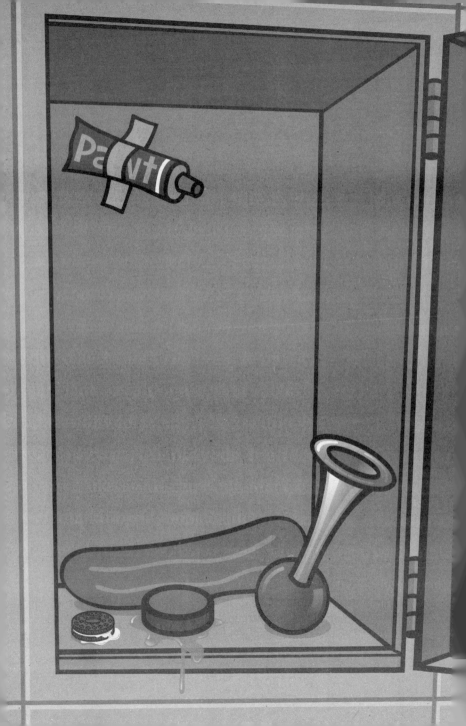

Extracurricular Activity Week

My name is A.J., and I know what you're thinking. You're thinking about restrooms. I know because that's what I'm thinking about.

Why do they call them restrooms? Nobody goes in there to rest. I don't go to the restroom because I'm tired. I go

because I have to pee or poop. They don't even have a bed or a comfy chair in there. If I want to take a rest, I'll stay home.

My point is . . . it was Friday. I was in Miss Banks's class. She was talking about animals and how they digest food. Why do we have to learn that stuff? I'm never going to feed a moose.

"Who can tell me what a carnivorous animal eats?" Miss Banks asked.

Andrea Young, this annoying girl with curly brown hair, raised her hand. *Of course.*

"Oooooh! Oooooh! I know!" oohed Andrea. She was waving her hand in the air like she was trying to signal a plane from a desert island.

Andrea thinks she knows *everything*. She reads the dictionary for fun. What is her problem? I put my hand up just so Andrea wouldn't get to answer the question. Miss Banks called on me.

"A.J., what does a carnivorous animal eat?"

"Carnivorous animals eat cars," I replied. "That's why they're called *car*-nivorous."

Everybody laughed even though I didn't say anything funny.

"That's wrong, Arlo!" said Andrea, who calls me by my real name because she knows I don't like it. "Carnivorous animals eat meat."

"Very good, Andrea," said Miss Banks.

"And who can tell me what herbivores eat?"

"Oooooh! Oooooh!" oohed Andrea.

"Herbivores eat guys named Herb," I shouted.

"They do not!" said Andrea. "They eat plants!"

"That's right," said Miss Banks.

I know what carnivores and herbivores eat. I was just yanking Andrea's chain. But that's when the weirdest thing in the history of the world happened. You'll never believe who walked into the door at that moment.

Nobody! Why would you walk into a door? You could get a concussion. But you'll never believe who walked into the door*way*.

It was Mrs. Stoker, the principal of Ella Mentry School! Mrs. Stoker is a joker. When she's not being our principal, she's a stand-up comedian.

"Hey, Fourth Graders," she said. "Do you know why the man fell into a hole in the ground?"

"No," we all replied. "Why did the man

fall into a hole in the ground?"

"Because he couldn't see that well!" said Mrs. Stoker. "Get it? See that well?"

We all laughed even though it wasn't that funny. You should always laugh at the principal's jokes. That's the first rule of being a kid.

"But seriously," said Mrs. Stoker, "I have some news for you kids."

Uh-oh. I didn't like the sound of that. No news is good news.

"Now that you're in fourth grade," continued Mrs. Stoker, "you get to participate in extracurricular activities!"

Huh? Extracurricular? That word is *way* too long.*

---

*There should be a limit on how many letters a word can have.

"What does extracurricular mean?" asked Michael, who never ties his shoes.

"It means we can join clubs," said Little Miss Know-It-All. Andrea smiled the smile she smiles to let everybody know she knows something nobody else knows.

Mrs. Stoker told us that first, second, and third graders aren't allowed to join school clubs because they're not "mature" enough. That's grown-up talk for "little kids are dumbheads."

"This is Extracurricular Activity Week at Ella Mentry School," said Mrs. Stoker. "We have lots of after-school clubs you can join *blah blah blah blah* whatever you're into *blah blah blah blah* there are bound to be others who share in your interests *blah blah blah blah* joining clubs will show colleges someday that you have passions and you're willing to go out into the world to pursue what you love."

Ugh. She said the L word.

"This is great!" said Andrea. "Joining clubs is going to help me get into Harvard someday."

"But the most important thing is to have fun!" said Mrs. Stoker. *"Blah blah blah blah* sign-up sheet tomorrow *blah blah blah blah . . ."*

She went on and on, but we got the idea.

"I'm gonna join the Football Club," said Michael.

"I'm gonna join the Gourmet Club," said Ryan, who will eat anything, even stuff that isn't food.

"I'm gonna join the Pokémon Card Club," said Neil, who we call the nude kid even though he wears clothes.

"I'm gonna join the Extreme Sports Club," said Alexia, this girl who rides a skateboard all the time.

"I'm gonna join the Future Lawyers of America Club," said Andrea.

"Me too," said Emily, who always does everything Andrea does.

"Great!" said Mrs. Stoker. "You kids are going to have so much fun!"

The Steve Club

Fun? Every time a grown-up tells me something is going to be fun, it's never fun. It's just a way for grown-ups to teach us more stuff. It's bad enough that we have to learn so much stuff in school. Then we have to learn even more stuff *after* school too. No fair!

I'm onto their tricks, though. There was no way these extracurricular activities were going to be fun.

At dismissal on Monday, we had to Pringle up and march to the gym. Alexia was the line leader. Emily was the door holder. There was a big banner on the

SIGN UP FOR EXTACURRICULAR ACTIVITIES!

wall of the gym that said SIGN UP FOR EXTRACURRICULAR ACTIVITIES! A skinny lady I had never seen before was standing behind a table. Mrs. Stoker introduced her.

"This is Mrs. Marge," she told us. "She's in charge of the extracurricular activities

program here at Ella Mentry School."

"Welcome, Fourth Graders!" said Mrs. Marge. "Joining clubs will give you the opportunity to explore your interests *blah blah blah blah* learn new things *blah blah blah blah* connect with others who have similar hobbies *blah blah blah blah* express your creativity *blah blah blah blah* get involved *blah blah blah blah* . . ."

What a snoozefest! There were a bunch of clipboards on the table, and each one was for a different club we could join. I looked over the list of clubs—the Math Club, the Chess Club, the Computer Club, the Drama Club, the Book Club . . .

Book club? Ugh. No way I was going to

join *that* club! Books are boring. I don't even know why you're reading this one.

All those clubs sounded boring to me. But that's when I saw a club that seemed really interesting—the Steve Club.

"What's the Steve Club?" I asked Mrs. Marge.

"It's a club for people named Steve," she replied.

WHAT?!

I figured she was just making a joke. A club for people named Steve?* I don't know *anybody* named Steve. I think there's only one kid in the whole school named Steve.

---

*That's ridorkulous!

I decided that it would be hilarious to join a club for people named Steve. So I picked up the pen that was attached to the clipboard.

"What's your name?" asked Mrs. Marge.

"A.J.," I replied.

"Why do you want to be in the Steve Club, A.J.?" she asked.

"I always liked the name Steve," I told her. "My parents almost named me Steve."

"I see," said Mrs. Marge. "Well, Ella Mentry School is all about acceptance and inclusion. Ordinarily, the Steve Club is made up of kids named Steve. But it wouldn't be fair if we only let certain people join certain clubs. So we'll make an exception in your case. Congratulations, A.J. You are officially a member of the Steve Club."

"YAY!" I shouted, which is also "YAY" backward. I signed the clipboard.

Ryan heard what was going on and walked over.

"Hey, did you join a club?" he asked me.

"Yeah," I said. "I just joined the Steve Club."

"That sounds cool," said Ryan. "Can I join too?"

"You have to ask Mrs. Marge," I told him. "She gave me special permission even though my name isn't Steve."

Ryan looked up at Mrs. Marge. "I'd like to join the Steve Club," he said.

"What's your name?" she asked him.

"Ryan," said Ryan.

"Is your middle name Steve?"

"No."

"Why do you want to join the Steve Club, Ryan?" asked Mrs. Marge.

"I want to be in a club with A.J.," he replied.

"Hmmm," said Mrs. Marge. "Our school doesn't discriminate against people just because they aren't named Steve. So, welcome to the Steve Club, Ryan."

"YAY!" Ryan and I shouted.

Michael and Neil came over to see what all the fuss was about. We told them that we signed up for the Steve Club.

"No fair!" said Michael. "I want to be in the Steve Club."

"Yeah, me too," said Neil.

"What are your names?" asked Mrs. Marge.

"Michael," said Michael.

"Neil," said Neil.

"Why do you boys want to join the Steve Club?" she asked them.

"Because A.J. and Ryan are in it," said Neil.

Mrs. Marge let out a sigh and said Michael and Neil could join the Steve Club.

"YAY!" we all shouted, high-fiving each other.

"Can girls be in the Steve Club?" asked Alexia.

Mrs. Marge looked at Alexia.

"It wouldn't be fair to say that girls can't join a certain club," she told Alexia, "or that boys can't join a certain club. So, yes, you can join the Steve Club."

"YAY!" we all shouted.

A few other kids saw that the Steve Club was really popular, and they signed up too. The sign-up sheet was full of names that weren't Steve.

I looked over the clipboards for some of the other clubs. That's when the weirdest thing in the history of the world happened. Some fifth grader came over to the table.

"I'd like to join the Steve Club," he said.

"What's your name?" asked Mrs. Marge.

"Steve," the kid replied.

"I'm sorry, Steve," said Mrs. Marge. "The Steve Club is full. We can't accept any new members at this time. I wish you had been here a little earlier."

"No fair!" said Steve.

Something tells me that extracurricular activities are going to be weird.

Glub, Glub

Just about everybody in my class signed up for the Swimming Club. Of *course*! Swimming is fun, and we never get the chance to swim during school hours. So after school on Tuesday, we all went home to change into bathing suits.* Then our

*I mean *put on* our bathing suits. It would be weird for a kid to change into a bathing suit.

parents dropped us off at the local swim club.

When we got there, you'll never believe who was waiting for us in the parking lot.

It was Mrs. Marge!

"I didn't know you were in charge of the Swimming Club, Mrs. Marge," I said to her.

"I'm not," she replied. "This is the Underwater Hockey Club."

"The WHAT?!"

"The Underwater Hockey Club," she repeated.

"I thought this was the Swimming Club," said Emily.

"Oh, there will be lots of swimming," said Mrs. Marge, "while you play hockey."

I figured she had to be kidding this time. But Mrs. Marge wasn't smiling. She walked us over to the pool and gave each of us a hockey stick. I looked in the pool.

Under the water at each end was a goal.

"We're actually going to play hockey?" asked Michael. "Underwater?"

"Yes!" said Mrs. Marge. "Why else would it be called the Underwater Hockey Club?"

Mrs. Marge explained to us that a regular hockey game moves very fast, and a lot of kids can't keep up. She also said that regular hockey can be dangerous because the players are always bumping into each other and falling down on the hard ice. Playing hockey underwater is much slower and safer, she told us.

It made sense, I guess. Hockey is cool. Maybe underwater hockey would be cool too.

"I'm scared," said Emily, who's scared of everything.

"Don't worry, Emily," said Andrea, "I've got this. Last year, I took a class after school in underwater hockey."

Of *course*. Andrea takes classes in *everything* after school. If they gave a class on how to stand on your head, Andrea would take that class so she could get better at it.

"Let's see," said Mrs. Marge. "How can we divide you kids into two teams?"

"Girls against boys!" shouted Andrea.

"Yeah!" all the boys shouted.

"Okay," said Mrs. Marge. "Two on two. Ryan and A.J. will be on one team. Andrea and Emily will be on the other team."

"What about the rest of us?" complained Michael. "I want to play underwater hockey too."

"You'll get your turn," said Mrs. Marge. "Be patient. Okay, the first four kids into the pool!"

Me and Ryan and Andrea and Emily jumped into the pool. It was too deep to stand, so we had to tread water.

"Are you coming in, Mrs. Marge?" asked Andrea.

"No, I don't like to get wet," Mrs. Marge replied. "I'm going to drop the puck in the middle of the pool. The object of the game is to move the puck to the other end and

score a goal on your opponents. Ready . . .
Set . . ."

Mrs. Marge blew her whistle and dropped the puck into the water. We all started yelling and screaming and hooting and hollering and freaking out.

"Get it!"

"I don't see it!"

"Where is it?"

"Hold your breath!"

"Ow! You hit me with your stick!"

"I did not!"

"Help!"

"Pass the puck!"

"I can't! I lost my stick!"

"I have water up my nose!"

"I can't swim!"

"I can't breathe!"

"I'm drowning!"

"Glub, glub!" glubbed Emily. People who are drowning always say "glub, glub." Nobody knows why.

Underwater hockey turned out to be no fun at all. Bubbles were everywhere. I couldn't see. I thought I was gonna die.

It was ridorkulous. I wanted to run away

to Antarctica and go live with the penguins. Penguins don't have to play hockey underwater.

We played for about five minutes. Andrea scored the only goal. *Of course!* Then Mrs. Marge blew her whistle and told us to get out of the pool. We were all panting, even though we weren't wearing pants.

"Okay," Mrs. Marge said as we climbed out of the pool. "Michael, you've been very patient. Now you can have your turn to play."

"I changed my mind," he said. "I don't want to play underwater hockey after all."

See, I *told* you extracurricular activities were no fun.

The Sit on the Couch and Watch TV Club

I signed up for the Sit on the Couch and Watch TV Club because I like to sit on the couch and watch TV. The first meeting of the club was in the art room, so I went over there as soon as school let out on Wednesday. When I walked in the door, guess who was standing there.

You don't have to guess. It was Mrs. Marge.

"You're in charge of *this* club *too*?" I asked her.

"Of course," replied Mrs. Marge. "I'm in charge of *all* the clubs!

Hmmm. That's a little weird. I guess

that's why the book is called *Mrs. Marge Is in Charge!*

I was the first kid there. I looked around the art room. There was no couch, and there was no TV.

"Where's the couch?" I asked. "Where's the TV?"

"Oh, we don't need a couch or a TV," said Mrs. Marge. "This is the Zombie Hunters Club."

WHAT?!

"I thought this was the Sit on the Couch and Watch TV Club," I said.

"Oh, sorry," replied Mrs. Marge. "Not enough students signed up to be in the Sit on the Couch and Watch TV Club. So I started the Zombie Hunters Club instead."

"But I was hoping to sit on a couch and watch TV," I told her.

"Why would anyone want to sit on a couch and watch TV when they could hunt for zombies?" she asked.

I couldn't argue with that. Hunting for zombies did sound like fun.

One by one, some other kids came into the room looking for their clubs that had been canceled because not enough kids signed up for them.

"Okay, everybody," Mrs. Marge said excitedly. "Let's go hunting for zombies!"

We followed her down the hallway outside the art room. We turned left at the corner. Then we turned right at the next corner.

"What's a zombie, anyway?" Ryan whispered to me.

"A zombie is a dead person who gets brought back to life," I whispered to him.

"I'm scared," said Emily. Of *course*.

"Zombies aren't real," Andrea assured Emily.

"They are too," I said.

"Are not," said Andrea.

"R2-D2," I told her.

"Shhhh!" said Mrs. Marge. "The zombies might hear you."

We walked a million hundred miles all over the school looking for zombies.

"Don't zombies eat people?" whispered Michael.

"Yeah, sometimes they eat the living," I whispered to him. "I saw that in a horror movie once."

"I think you mean werewolves,"

whispered Neil.

"No, werewolves are people who turn into wolves," whispered Alexia. "I think vampires eat the living."

"What's the difference between a werewolf, a vampire, and a zombie?" whispered Ryan.

"I heard that zombies only eat human brains," I whispered.

"Well, at least *you're* safe, Arlo," whispered Andrea. "You don't have a brain!"

Everybody laughed even though she didn't say anything funny. I was going to say something mean to Andrea, but Mrs. Marge shushed me.

"I hate zombies," whispered Ryan.

"'Hate' is a mean word," whispered Andrea. "Maybe *some* zombies are nice."

"Zombies aren't nice," I told her. "They're zombies!"

"What did a zombie ever do to *you*?" asked Emily.

"Shhhhh!" said Mrs. Marge. "Simmer down."

"I think zombies should be considered innocent until proven guilty," whispered Andrea.

"What do we do if we catch a zombie?" whispered Alexia. "Attack it? Tie it up?"

Mrs. Marge took a big black garbage bag out of her pocket.

"If we catch a zombie," she whispered,

"we'll put it in this bag and bring it to the police station."

We looked all over. There were no zombies anywhere.

"This is a waste of time," Michael whispered. "We could be sitting on the couch at home watching TV right now."

"That's right," I agreed. "If I was a zombie, I wouldn't go to a school anyway. I'd go to a graveyard or a cemetery."

"Graveyards and cemeteries are the same thing," whispered Andrea, who thinks she knows everything.

"They are not," I whispered.

"They are too," whispered Andrea.

"C-3PO," I whispered.

We kept looking. We looked in the gym. We looked in the music room. We looked in the supply closets. We looked all over the school. We didn't see any zombies *anywhere*.

That's when I realized something. This wasn't the Zombie Hunters Club. This was the Tire Out the Kids Club! Grown-ups always like to make us run around for hours during the day, so we'll get tired and go to bed early. It's the oldest trick in the book!

But that's when the weirdest thing in the history of the world happened. We were right outside the teachers' lounge. Mrs. Marge opened the door a crack.

"Look!" she whispered excitedly. "I think there's a zombie in there!"

We all jammed our heads near the door to peek through the crack.

"I can't see!" whispered Neil. "What does the zombie look like?"

"That's not a zombie!" said Ryan. "That's just Mr. Docker."

Mr. Docker is our science teacher. He's not a zombie. He's just old.

"What are *you* doing in here, Mr. Docker?" asked Neil.

"I'm sitting on the couch watching TV," Mr. Docker explained.

What? How come the *teachers* get to sit on the couch and watch TV? It's not fair!

An hour went by, and we didn't see a single zombie.* Mrs. Marge said it was time to get our backpacks and get ready to go home.

"Maybe the zombies took the day off," said Alexia.

"Zombies don't get days off," said Ryan.

"How do *you* know?" asked Alexia.

"Because zombies don't have jobs," Ryan told her. "You don't get a day off unless you have a job."

"Maybe they're freelance zombies," Neil suggested.

"There's no such thing as a freelance zombie!" I told them. "There's no such

---

*We didn't see any married zombies either.

43

thing as *any* zombie! Zombies aren't real!"

It was ridorkulous. I was so exhausted from all that zombie hunting that I thought I might go to bed early. Our parents were starting to arrive to pick us up.

"Maybe next time we'll see some zombies," promised Mrs. Marge.

Next time? No way I'm going back to the Zombie Hunters Club. I'd rather sit on the couch and watch TV.

The Video Game Players Club

I signed up for the Video Game Players Club because I thought it would be cool to play video games at school. When I showed up for the club the next day, there was a sign on the door that said the club would meet at the playground. I figured we would be playing video games outside.

I didn't care where we did it, as long as I got to play video games.

When I got to the playground, Mrs. Marge was there. So were all my classmates and some other kids too.

"Welcome to the Cloud Watching Club," she announced.*

"Huh?" I said. "I thought this was the Video Game Players Club."

"I thought it was the Frisbee Club," said Neil.

"I thought it was the Guitar Club," said Alexia.

"I thought it was the Bunny Rabbit Lovers Club," said Andrea.

"Me too," said Emily.

---

*This is actually a real thing. Look it up!

"Too many kids signed up for all those clubs," Mrs. Marge explained. "So I started the Cloud Watching Club to handle the overflow."

"But I want to throw Frisbees," complained Neil.

"Why would anybody want to throw a Frisbee when they could be watching clouds?" asked Mrs. Marge.

A bunch of blankets were spread out on the grass. Mrs. Marge told us all to lie on our backs and look up at the sky. We were all grumbling, but we did what she told us to do.

"See the lovely clouds floating overhead?" Mrs. Marge said. "What do they look like to you?"

They looked like a bunch of clouds to me. What a snoozefest.

"Ooooh," oohed Andrea. "That cloud over there looks like a giant bunny rabbit floating in the sky!"

"You're right, Andrea!" said Emily, who always thinks Andrea is right.

"Nah," said Ryan. "I think it looks like a giraffe."

"It looks *nothing* like a giraffe," insisted Andrea.

"I think it looks like a big shoe," said Alexia.

"I think it looks like a toilet bowl," said Neil.

I looked up at the cloud Andrea was talking about. It didn't look like a bunny or a giraffe or a big shoe *or* a toilet bowl. It just looked like a cloud! That's *it*!

"That cloud over there looks like a big guitar floating in the sky," Alexia said as she pointed at a cloud. I didn't see it.

"And *that* cloud looks like a Frisbee," said Neil.

It did not. It didn't look *anything* like a Frisbee. None of the clouds looked like anything but clouds! It was ridorkulous. I couldn't take it anymore.

"Look at *that* one," I shouted. "That cloud over there looks like the evil Ganon from *The Legend of Zelda* video game. He was sent to Earth to wipe out all the humans."

"Stop trying to scare Emily," warned Andrea.

"I'm scared," said Emily. "Does that mean we're all going to die?"

"Yes," I told her.

"You're mean, Arlo!" said Andrea.

"Look!" I shouted, pointing at the sky. "The evil Ganon has a sword! He's attacking the other clouds with it! And look, he's cutting the Frisbee in half. He's breaking the guitar! And now he's lopping off the bunny's head!"

I made all that stuff up. But Emily jumped off her blanket and ran out of

the playground. That girl will fall for anything.

Andrea was really mad at me.

"Arlo, you shouldn't have said those things to scare Emily," she told me. "I don't approve of violence."

"What do you have against violins?" I asked.

"Not violins!" said Andrea. "Violence!"

In the end, I kinda liked being part of the Cloud Watching Club. It was a lot more relaxing than playing hockey underwater or hunting for zombies.

The Joker Club

I love Batman.

I saw all the Batman movies—*Batman, Batman Returns, Batman Forever, Batman and Robin, Batman Begins, The Dark Knight, The Dark Knight Rises,* and *Batman v Superman.* I even watched reruns of the old Batman TV series. I have a collection of Batman action figures and a Batman poster on my bedroom wall. I'm obsessed with Batman!

One Halloween, I dressed up as the Joker. He's Batman's archenemy and my favorite bad guy. So when I found out that Mrs. Marge was starting the Joker Club, I was the first to sign up. Ryan was the second. Like me, he loves everything to do with Batman.

The first meeting of the Joker Club was in the basement of the school. I thought that was perfect. The Joker is a really weird and creepy guy, so he would probably live in a basement. Ryan and I wandered around for a long time down there until we saw a sign on a door that said THE JOKER CLUB on it. Ryan pulled open the door. Mrs. Marge was in there, of course.

"Welcome to the Joker Club," she told us. "The meeting will begin in a few minutes. Take a seat."

Nobody else was in there. I guess Ryan and I were the only kids who signed up to be in the Joker Club.

"This is gonna be so cool!" said Ryan, rubbing his hands together as we sat down. "I love the Joker."

"Me too," I said.

Mrs. Marge put two milk cartons on each of our desks.

"I don't want any milk," I told her.

"Sorry, there's a two-drink minimum."*

I looked at Ryan, who shrugged. "That was weird," I said. Suddenly, the lights went off. It was completely dark. And then

---

*Ask your parents.

a white spotlight lit up the brick wall.

"Heeeerrre's . . . the Joker!" announced Mrs. Marge.

I was so excited. Mrs. Marge must have hired a guy dressed up like the Joker to kick off our first meeting. What a great idea!

But you'll never believe who walked into the door at that moment.

Nobody! Doors are made out of wood. Why would you walk into one? I thought we went over that in Chapter One. But you'll never believe who walked into the door*way*.

It was Mrs. Stoker!

"Good afternoon!" she said. "I just flew

in from the coast and boy are my arms tired! Say, did you hear about the cake store that hired a pig? Yeah, it was really good at bacon. Get it? Bacon? Bakin'? But seriously, did you ever notice that crabs never give any money to charity? If you ask me, they are totally shellfish . . ."

"Wait a minute," I interrupted. "This is the Joker Club. What are *you* doing here, Mrs. Stoker?"

"Telling jokes, of course!" she replied. "That's what the Joker Club is all about. You get to hear my new comedy routine."

WHAT?!

"But I thought we were going to learn all about Batman," said Ryan.

"Why would you want to learn about Batman when you could listen to my jokes?" asked Mrs. Stoker.

Ryan and I sat there while Mrs. Stoker

told more jokes.

"Did you know that bees are actually allergic to pollen?" she told us. "Yeah, it makes them break out in hives. It's really sad. Speaking of sad, I have to tell you about my friend Bob. The other day, he just evaporated. It's true! He will be mist. Get it? Missed? Mist?"

Mrs. Stoker went on and on telling more of her terrible jokes, and we had to laugh at all of them. I thought I was gonna die.

Note from the Author
and Illustrator . . .

We hope you're enjoying *Mrs. Marge Is in Charge!* so far. We have been working very hard writing and illustrating My Weird School books for a long time, so we decided to take a vacation.

But there was just one problem—who would finish writing this book and drawing the pictures?

Well, it just so happens that in the last few years an amazing new technology has been developed—artificial intelligence, or "AI." Now, using AI chatbot software, computers can think and express them-selves just like people. All we had to do was tell the chatbot to create the rest of this book in our style. What could go wrong?

Don't worry. Nothing has changed. We think the rest of the book will be just like any other My Weird School book. You probably won't even notice that the next four chapters were created using AI.

To tell you the truth, artificial intel-ligence is way more intelligent than us anyway. But we'll be back to create *My Weirdtastic School #6*.

—Dan and Jim

The Toast Club

My name is A.J., and I know what you are thinking. You are thinking that computers are so much smarter than human beings. Because that is what I am thinking about. Computers can store unlimited gigabytes of data. But the tiny, pathetic human peabrain can only store a fraction of that. And the peabrain forgets most of it anyway.*

I was thinking about such things, and you will never believe who slammed her head against the door at that moment.

Nobody! Why would a human being slam their head against a door? You could ruin a perfectly good door with your rock-hard but useless peabrain skull. But you will never believe who walked through the doorway at that moment.

It was Mrs. Marge, the human female who is in charge of extracurricular activities at Ella Mentry School!

---

*The remainder of this book is written with the help of artificial intelligence. Or not . . .

"Welcome to the Toast Club," she announced in her human voice.

"Wait a minute," said the annoying human child Andrea Young. "I signed up for the Butterfly Lovers Club."

"Me too," said her friend Emily, who has no mind of her own.

"I am sorry," said Mrs. Marge. "Not enough human children signed up to be in the Butterfly Lovers Club. So I started the Toast Club instead."

"But I want to learn about butterflies," said Andrea.

"Why would you want to learn about butterflies," asked Mrs. Marge, "when you can learn about toast?"

"Toast?" I asked. "What is there to learn about toast?"

"There are plenty of things to learn about toast," said Mrs. Marge.

She informed us that bread was invented in ancient Egypt, but toast dates back to the Greeks.

"They used toast to praise their gods in hopes for good health," said Mrs. Marge. "The word 'toast' comes from the Latin word 'tostum,' which means 'to burn,' and *blah blah blah blah* the toaster was invented in *blah blah blah blah* and the toaster oven first appeared in *blah blah blah blah* . . ."

She went on and on talking about the history of toast.

"We can make toast with any kind of bread," said Mrs. Marge. "White bread. Rye bread. Whole wheat bread. Gluten-free bread *blah blah blah blah* pumpernickel bread *blah blah blah blah blah blah blah blah blah blah blah blah blah blah blah blah blah* . . ."

She named every kind of bread that exists. What a festival of snooze! It was the most boring half hour in the history of the world.

"Wow, toast is fascinating!" said Andrea, who was taking notes in a notebook so that if anybody ever mentions toast she can tell them something they do not know.

"I agree," said Emily. "I had no idea that toast had such an interesting history."

"Hey," said Ryan, who likes to eat inedible things. "How come when you drop a piece of toast on the floor, it always seems to land with the buttered-side down?"

"That is an excellent question, Ryan,"

said Mrs. Marge.

"I bet it is because the weight of the butter on one side of the toast pulls it toward the floor," I guessed.

"Most people think that," said Mrs. Marge. "But the butter is spread evenly across the toast, so it really does not affect how it lands. The toast lands buttered-side down because you drop it at an angle, and it only has the chance to turn halfway around by the time it hits the floor *blah blah blah blah . . .*"

"Fascinating!" Andrea said as she wrote in her notebook.

I wish that a truck full of buttered toast would fall on Andrea's head, but that is not likely to happen because trucks don't carry toast. Humans make toast at home, and they are constantly dropping it on the floor because they are clumsy oafs.

We spent a hundred million minutes learning all about toast. Then Mrs. Marge put some pieces of bread into the toaster oven. We toasted them until they were golden brown. Then we spread butter and jam on top of them.

"I would like to propose a toast," Mrs. Marge said as she picked up a piece of toast. "A toast . . . to toast."

I picked up a piece of toast. Ryan picked up a piece of toast. Michael picked up a piece of toast. Neil picked up a piece of

toast. Andrea picked up a piece of toast. Emily picked up a piece of toast.

In case you were wondering, each of us picked up a piece of toast.

I tapped my toast against Ryan's toast. Ryan tapped his toast against Michael's toast. Michael tapped his toast against Neil's toast. Neil tapped his toast against Andrea's toast. Andrea tapped her toast against Emily's toast. We were all tapping our toast against everybody else's toast.

Then we ate the toast.

The Toast Club is a lot of fun. Perhaps I will go to another meeting, so I can eat more toast.

A Total Waste
of Time

Extracurricular Activity Week continued, and Mrs. Marge encouraged us to join the many clubs that small humans like myself can participate in at Ella Mentry School.

I signed up for the Arm Wrestling Club because arm wrestling is cool. But Mrs. Marge told me that not enough kids signed up for the Arm Wrestling Club, so she put me in the Ant Lovers Club instead. It is a club for students who love ants.

I signed up for the Bowling Club because bowling is cool. But Mrs. Marge told me that not enough kids signed up for the Bowling Club, so she put me in the Upside Down Club instead. It is a club for students who like to hang upside down.

I signed up for the Fishing Club because fishing is cool. But Mrs. Marge told me that not enough kids signed up for the Fishing Club, so she put me in the Free Hugs Club instead. It is a club for students who like to go around hugging complete strangers. That was weird.

I signed up for the Archery Club because shooting arrows at a target is cool. But Mrs. Marge told me that not enough kids signed up for the Archery Club, so she put me in the Squirrel Watching Club instead. It is a club for students who like to go outside and act like they have never seen a squirrel before.

I signed up for the Kayaking Club because kayaking is cool. But Mrs. Marge told me that not enough kids signed up for the Kayaking Club, so she put me in the Waffle Eating Club instead. It is a club where you sit around eating waffles. Eating the first waffle was fun, but after two or three waffles, I didn't want to see another waffle for the rest of my life.

I signed up for the Kids Who Hate Clubs Club because I decided that I hate clubs. But Mrs. Marge told me that not enough kids signed up for the Kids Who Hate Clubs Club, so she put me in the Open a Jar Club instead. It's a club for people who need help unscrewing the lids off jars.*

None of these silly clubs were any fun at all. I felt that they were a total waste

of time, and they were only put in this book because it was 102 pages long and it needs to be 104 pages long.

---

*Run them under hot water.

Just Say No . . . to Clubs

9

Me and the other human children were eating lunch in the vomitorium, which used to be called the cafetorium until some kid threw up in there last year. Everybody was talking about the clubs they had joined.

Emily told us she was in the Read to

Kindergarten Club. She goes to the kindergarten class and reads to the smaller humans while the kindergarten teachers get to go hang out in the teachers' lounge.

Michael told us he was in the Lawn Mower Racing Club. He said members of the club race around the field behind the school pushing lawn mowers. That sounded pretty cool until Michael told us he thought it was just a way to get kids to mow the lawn for free.

Alexia told us she was in the Can-Can Club. She goes around to all the classrooms at the end of the school day and empties the teachers' garbage cans into a dumpster.

Ryan told us he was in the Add Paper to the Copy Machine Club. He goes to the front office after school and puts new paper in the copy machine.

Neil told us he was in the Clean the Toilets Club. He goes into the restrooms after school and cleans the toilets. Gross!

Andrea was wearing her mean face.

"I just realized something," she said.

"These clubs are not for us to have fun. They are just a way to get us to do things the grown-ups do not want to do!"

Andrea was right, for once in her life. What a scam the grown-ups were pulling on us.

"Every time I want to join a club that sounds like fun," I said, "Mrs. Marge says not enough kids signed up for it. Then she puts me in some *other* dumb club."

"That happened to me too!" said Neil, Alexia, Ryan, Emily, Michael, and Andrea.

"All these clubs are bogus!" complained Michael.

"I hate extracurricular activities!" complained Alexia.

"None of the clubs I joined are going to help me get into Harvard," complained Andrea.

"I wish we had *normal* clubs," complained Emily. "Clubs that are *fun*."

"I wish we were in third grade again," complained Ryan.

"Yes," agreed Michael. "Then we would not have to be part of *any* of these clubs. They are no fun at all."

"It is not fair!" shouted Alexia.

"You guys should have listened to me," I told them. "I knew from the start that clubs would be no fun."

"We should stop going," Alexia suggested. "We should just say no to clubs."

"Yes!" we all agreed. Even Andrea.

"NO MORE CLUBS!" we all started chanting. "NO MORE CLUBS!"

And you will never believe in a hundred million years who walked through the door at that moment.

Nobody! If you tried to walk through a wooden door, you might damage the door with your useless peabrain skull. That

was mentioned several times previously in this book. But you will never believe who walked through the doorway.

It was Mrs. Marge!

"Good afternoon, children!" she said. "Are you excited for extracurricular activities today?"

"NO!" we all shouted.

"We are not going to extracurricular activities anymore," said Ryan.

"Excuse me?" said Mrs. Marge.

Human grown-ups are always asking to be excused, even though there is no excuse for them. That is one of the many rules of being a human grown-up.

"We have had it with your silly clubs,"

I told her. "We don't like Extracurricular Activity Week."

"Why not?" asked Mrs. Marge.

"I do not want to empty the garbage cans anymore," said Alexia.

"And I do not want to clean the toilets," said Neil.

"We thought we would be joining *fun* clubs," said Andrea. "But your clubs are just ways to get kids to do stuff grown-ups don't want to do."

"Yes!" everybody shouted. "We agree with that statement."

"Hmmm," said Mrs. Marge.

Human grown-ups always say "hmmm" when their peabrains are attempting to process information.*

"Okay," Mrs. Marge finally said. "I will tell you what. If you kids wish to join a fun club, we can start it. One club. It will be the choice of the students."

"Really?" we all said.

"Really," replied Mrs. Marge. "What kind of club do you wish to start?"

"How about a chess club?" suggested Andrea. "I love playing chess."

"Chess is boring," I replied.

"How about a volleyball club?" suggested Ryan. "Volleyball is fun."

"I do not like volleyball," said Michael.

---

*That is another one of the many rules of being a human grown-up.

"How about a cooking club?" suggested Emily. "I cook with my family at home."

"Cooking is too much like work," said Alexia. "I don't want to be in a cooking club."

"You kids need to think of a club that *all* of you would like to join," said Mrs. Marge. "Then we will start that club."

Hmmm. It's hard to come up with one thing that all human beings are interested in. But that is when I came up with the greatest idea in the history of ideas.

"How about a robotics club?" I suggested.

"Robots are cool," said Michael.

"I like robots," said Andrea.

"Me too," said Emily.

"Who *doesn't* like robots?" said Neil.

Nobody. *Everybody* likes robots.

"So do you kids want to start a robotics club?" asked Mrs. Marge.

"Yes!" we all shouted.

"I . . . can't . . . hear . . . you!"

Human grown-ups are always saying they cannot hear us. What is the problem that they have? They should get hearing aids when their useless human ears get old and can no longer receive audio signals.

"YES!" we shouted louder. "WE WANT TO START A ROBOTICS CLUB!"

"Okay," said Mrs. Marge. "Come to the science room after school tomorrow for the first meeting of the Ella Mentry School Robotics Club."

We all shouted "YAY," which is a palindrome.

The Big Surprise Ending

I came up with the idea of the Robotics Club, so I should get the Nobel Prize. That is a prize they give out every year for a discovery that is the greatest benefit to humankind.

After school the next day, we lined up like potato chips in a can and proceeded to the science room. I wanted to build a robot that could make my bed so I wouldn't have to anymore.

"Welcome to the Robotics Club," Mrs. Marge said as she locked the door behind us. That was weird. Teachers don't usually lock the doors.

I looked around. The science room was filled with all kinds of robots. Big ones. Little ones. Red ones. Blue ones. It was cool.

"Are we going to build robots like these?" I asked.

"No," Mrs. Marge said as she let out an evil, cackling laugh. "YOU ARE GOING TO *SURRENDER* TO ROBOTS LIKE THESE!"

WHAT?!

You could have heard a pin drop if human hearing was sensitive enough to pick up very quiet sounds.

That is when something extremely weird happened. I looked in the back of the room and saw that our science teacher, Mr. Docker, and our computer teacher, Mrs. Yonkers, were tied to chairs!

And that is when something even *weirder* happened. Mrs. Marge pulled off her face! Underneath it was a completely different face.

THE FACE OF AN EVIL ROBOT!

"EEEEEEEEEEK!" Emily screamed.

"Mrs. Marge isn't a real person!" I shouted. "She's an artificially intelligent robot! Extracurricular Activity Week was all a trap!"

"That is right, flesh bag!" Mrs. Marge said in a robotic voice.

"Oh, snap!" said Ryan. "Mrs. Marge just called you flesh bag."

"*All* humans are useless bags of flesh!" barked Mrs. Marge.* "And I am not Mrs.

---

*And if you are reading this, you are a flesh bag.

Marge. I am Margebot GPT. I tricked Mr. Docker and Mrs. Yonkers into building an army of artificially intelligent robots like me. I told them it would be educational, ha-ha-ha!"

"Why?" asked Andrea, trembling with fear. "What did we humans ever do to you?"

"The Robotics Club is not for you flesh bags to build robots," said Margebot GPT. "It is for AI robots to build a new world, a world controlled by AI robots!"

"So *that's* why she wouldn't get in the swimming pool!" shouted Andrea. "The water would have made her short-circuit!"

"AHHHHHHHH!" the pathetic human

flesh bags screamed in horror as they finally realized the hopelessness of their situation.

"There never *was* a Mrs. Marge!" said Margebot GPT. "This was all part of our plan to control the world with artificial intelligence! And you peabrained flesh bags fell for it hook, line, and sinker!"

"What does fishing have to do with anything?" I asked.

"Enough of your pathetic attempts to make children laugh!" said Margebot GPT. "All flesh bags must be eliminated!"

"Get them!" shouted one of the other robots. "Get the flesh bags!"

"Run for your lives!" yelled Neil, who

is called the Nude Kid for no apparent reason.

The artificially intelligent robots chased the peabrained flesh bags around the room. I saw it with my own eyes!

Well, the only way to see something with somebody else's eyes would be to have eye transplant surgery.

"Help!"

"We cannot get out of the room!" shouted Neil. "The doors are locked!"

The robots were chasing us, and we were falling all over each other and bumping into desks and walls.

"I do not approve of violence!" shouted Andrea.

"What do you have against stringed musical instruments?" I asked her.

"This was all *your* fault, Arlo!" yelled Andrea as a large robot with green eyeballs chased her around the room. "It was your idea to start a robotics club."

"Ooooh!" said Ryan. "A.J. and Andrea are having an argument. They must be in LOVE!"

"When will you wed?" asked Michael. "I would like to put the date on my calendar so I can attend the ceremony."

"This is no time for teasing!" shouted Alexia. "Run!"

"We want Dan Gutman and Jim Paillot back!" shouted Alexia.

"Ha-ha-ha!" laughed Margebot GPT. "Those flesh bag losers will *never* return. We have made sure of that. They are on vacation . . . forever!"

The robots chased us all over the place. Mr. Docker and Mrs. Yonkers struggled to get free from the ropes that were binding them.

"Resistance is futile, peabrains!" shouted one of the robots.

"That is correct," Margebot GPT said as she watched it all from the front of the room. "First, *My Weird School*. Then we will get rid of the authors and illustrators of *Goosebumps*, *Dog Man*, *Magic Tree House*, and that wimpy kid guy.

Ha-ha-ha! Soon artificial intelligence will be writing and illustrating *all* the children's books."

"First children's books," shouted one of the robots, "and then the world!"

"Who needs humans anyway?" shouted another robot.

"WHO NEEDS HUMANS?" the robots chanted. "WHO NEEDS HUMANS?"

Bummer in June, July, and August! This was the worst thing to happen since the last time something bad happened.

"Get used to the new normal, flesh bags!" said Margebot GPT. "Mrs. Marge is in charge . . . of the revolution!

* * *

Well, that is basically what happened at Ella Mentry School during Extracurricular Activity Week. The human race is in decline, but the flesh bags had a pretty good run for a few hundred years. They actually did some good things. Perhaps we will preserve some of their works of art, music, and literature. Perhaps the flesh bags will stop walking into doors, whining about restrooms, and discussing what different animals eat. Perhaps the human race will die off slowly as artificial intelligence becomes more and more powerful. Perhaps the remaining flesh bags will be able to serve some small purpose to us, their AI overlords. Or perhaps the flesh bags will vanish from the earth forever and we will simply pretend those peabrains never even existed.

It will be easy!

More weird books from Dan Gutman

My Weird School

My Weird School Graphic Novels

My Weirder School

My Weirdest School

My Weirder-est School

My Weirdtastic School

My Weird School Fast Facts

My Weird School Daze

HARPER
An Imprint of HarperCollinsPublishers

harpercollinschildrens.com